NEW YORK TIMES BESTSELLING AUTHOR

DALE EARNHARDT JR.

NASCAR HALL OF FAMER

BUSTER GETS BACK ON TRACK

Illustrated by
ELA SMIETANKA

An Imprint of Thomas Nelson

Buster Gets Back on Track

Tommy Nelson, PO Box 141000, Nashville, TN 37214

Published in Nashville, Tennessee, by Tommy Nelson. Tommy Nelson is an imprint of Thomas Nelson. Thomas Nelson is a registered trademark of HarperCollins Christian Publishing, Inc.

Tommy Nelson titles may be purchased in bulk for educational, business, fund-raising, or sales promotional use. For information, please email SpecialMarkets@Tho masNelson.com.

ISBN 978-1-4002-4347-1 (audiobook)
ISBN 978-1-4002-4343-3 (eBook)
ISBN 978-1-4002-3337-3 (HC)
ISBN 978-1-4002-4745-5 (BAM signed ed.)

Library of Congress Cataloging-in-Publication Data is on file.

Written by Dale Earnhardt Jr. with Caryn Rivadeneira

Illustrated by Ela Smietanka

Printed in Malaysia

23 24 25 26 27 IMG 6 5 4 3 2 1

Mfr: IMG / Selangor, Malaysia / August 2023 / PO #12083244

E TEAMS

TEAM FAST LANE

KAT

After a career in the military, Kat started off-road racing and never looked back. Fans are used to seeing her pink-camouflage frame roar over anything that gets in her way.

GUS

Not to be outdone by his big sister, Gus joined Kat on the off-road racing track after his time in the service. He now spends his days covered in mud and wouldn't have it any other way.

SNEAK ATTACK RACING

SCUFF

Sneak Attack Racing's reigning star, Scuff, shows his sass on *and* off the track. He's quick on his tires—and with his sharp tongue. He's looking forward to making mischief at Racing School this year.

To our girls, Isla and Nicole.

Buster squealed into the final turn, just inches ahead of Click and Jimmy Jam.

I have to win! he thought to himself. *I can't lose again!* His cheeks turned red as he remembered the other four practice races he'd lost that morning.

But Jimmy Jam zoomed ahead with Click in his shadow.

Swoosh! The checkered flag waved as Jimmy Jam and Click whizzed across the finish line.

"Ugh," Buster moaned. "I was so close!"

"Super close," Jimmy Jam said with a wink. "You'll beat us by the end of Racing School."

"Speak for yourself," Click teased.

Buster sank onto the track. "Click's right. I'm never going to win."

"You just need to get a handle on your emotions," said Coach Hog, the leader of Buster's team, Punchy Motorsports. "Here's Racing School lesson *numero uno*:

Breathe in deep.
Count 1, 2, 3.
Breathe out slow.
And off you'll go!"

Coach Hog waved the green flag. Click sped ahead.

"Breathe in deep!" Coach Hog yelled as Buster **zoomed** past Jimmy Jam.

Click was just ahead. Buster shot forward.

"Breathe out slow," reminded Coach Hog.

"—or Buster's gonna blunder!" a voice cackled from the pit.

Oh no! Scuff!

Frustration coursed through Buster's engine, and as he zigzagged ahead, he forgot all about breathing.

Buster and Click were neck and neck.
Just a little more . . . A little more . . .
Splash!

Buster squinted at a water hose whipping wild and loose across the track. Click veered out of the way. But Buster panicked and thudded over the wild hose. It snaked around his tires and slowed him down.

Ugh! Another mistake! This can't be happening!

"Breathe in deep!" Coach Hog shouted as Buster struggled to catch Click.

"Ha-ha! You stink!" Scuff yelled.

At that, Buster gritted his teeth, *held* his breath, and roared *off* the track and away from Racing School.

Buster's heart pounded, and his mind raced as he flew down the road.

Why can't Scuff leave me alone? Why do I always mess up? Why can't I stop feeling this way? Why?!

Then something rumbled in the distance.

Buster slowed down. He turned onto a path through the woods, peeking through the gaps in the trees.

His eyes grew wide.

“Pretty cool, right?” said a voice from above.

Buster jumped. Two military vehicles towered over him. He gulped and deepened his voice. “Uh, yeah. Super cool. What is this?”

“Off-road racing,” the pink-camouflage Humvee said. “We’re on Team Fast Lane. We joined after the army. I’m Kat. This muddy guy is my brother, Gus.”

"I'm Buster. Can I try your off-road track?"

Gus nodded. "Roger that, little guy. Follow us."

They **rambled** over brambles, **crunched** over mulch, and **crashed** through wet grass until they reached the start of the racecourse.

Humvees crawled through swamps, over boulders, and up steep hills.

"They move pretty slow," Buster said.

"Off-road racing is about more than speed," Gus said.

Not for a race car, Buster thought. "Race ya!"

PUNCHY
MOTORSPORTS
8

Buster **splashed** into the swamp first. The mud stuck to his tires and slowed him down.

"Argh!" Buster yelled as Gus passed him.

Buster grunted his way out of the swamp, shook off the mud, and dashed past Gus toward the big hill.

Buster roared into the steep climb. He got halfway up and stopped.

He revved his engine—**vroom**, **vroom**—but his tires didn't budge.

Buster was stuck!

I keep messing up, and everyone saw it happen, Buster thought. *I give up! I can't do this anymore.*

Buster's emotions bubbled up until his eyes leaked tears. He reversed down the hill in front of his new friends, but he wouldn't look at them. Instead, he wiped his windshield and raced into the woods.

Buster's hood hung low as he crunched along the road. He kicked a rock. **Clink! Clink!**

"Careful," said a familiar voice. "I just got my doors decaled!"

"I've got a photo shoot later," said another.

"Calm down. Let's breathe in deep," laughed a big, booming voice.

Click!
Jimmy Jam!
Coach Hog!

Buster perked up. "How'd you find me?" he asked.

"We were worried, so we followed your tracks," Coach Hog said.

"There aren't many racing tires on this road," said Click as she blew the dust off her tires.

"Yeah, most are"—Jimmy Jam's mouth dropped as Kat and Gus rolled through the bushes and onto the road—"that size!"

"You stormed off before I could congratulate you!" Gus said.

"Congratulate? But I lost—like always." Buster sighed as Gus and Kat introduced themselves to the rest of the team.

"Nobody has ever climbed as high as you did on their first try," Kat said.

"He *flew* up that hill!" Gus told the others.

"But I got stuck," Buster admitted with a huff.

PUNCHY MOTORSPORTS
03
5

PUNCHY MOTORSPORTS
8
PUNCHY MOTORSPORTS
5
PUNCHY MOTORSPORTS
pit bull
GAS

"The problem is that your *feelings* got stuck," Kat said. "It's okay to try and fail."

"Or to get frustrated or embarrassed," Gus added.

"It's hard to imagine *you* embarrassed," Click said to Gus.

"You kidding?" Kat laughed. "Buster got stuck in a swamp and *still* beat Gus to the hill. Every Humvee back there was teasing my little bro."

"Sorry I embarrassed you," Buster said, stifling a laugh.

"It's cool," Gus said. "I just breathe in deep, try again, and focus on the road ahead."

"It's like I told you!" Coach Hog said. "It's normal to have big feelings. We just can't let our feelings control how we act."

Buster smiled, took a deep breath, and said, "Race ya!"

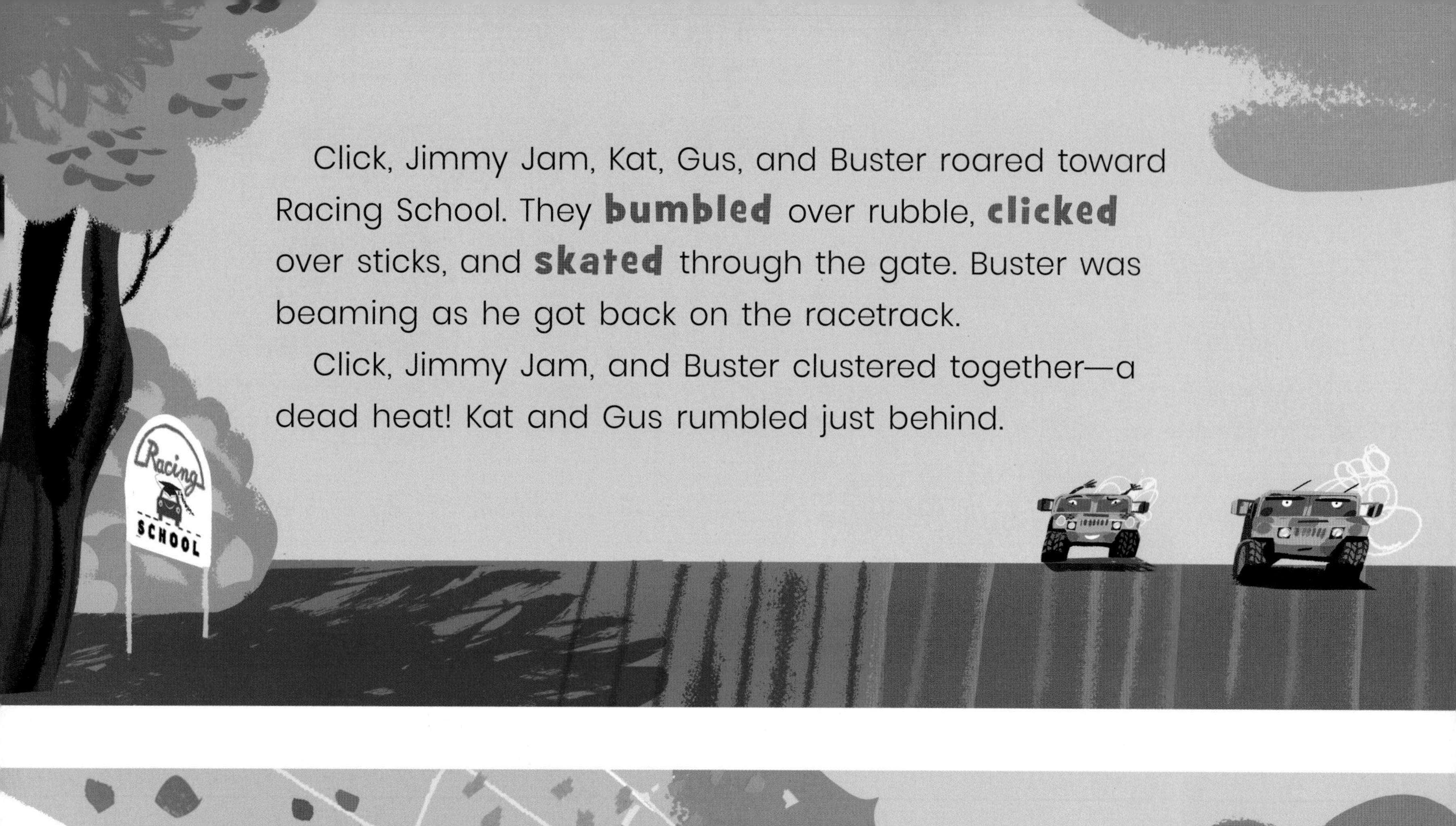

Click, Jimmy Jam, Kat, Gus, and Buster roared toward Racing School. They **bumbled** over rubble, **clicked** over sticks, and **skated** through the gate. Buster was beaming as he got back on the racetrack.

Click, Jimmy Jam, and Buster clustered together—a dead heat! Kat and Gus rumbled just behind.

As they rounded the final turn, Buster lost momentum. Scuff watched from pit road and yelled, “You’ll never make it, Buster Fluster!”

Buster’s stomach lurched. But he said to himself, *I’m not running away this time.*

ZOOM!

Buster took a moment to steady himself. *Okay, time to breathe in deep. Count 1, 2, 3. Breathe out slow. And off I go!*

It worked! Buster eyed the finish line and sped ahead.

Swoosh!

The checkered flag waved as Buster zipped across the finish line—with his teammates and new friends just behind.

The whole team cheered for Buster.

"I knew you'd win before the end of school," Jimmy Jam said with a wink.

Buster's smile was as wide as the track.

Winning felt great! But knowing he didn't have to get stuck in his feelings? Well, that felt even better.

BUSTER PRACTICES HIS BREATHING OFF THE TRACK

Honk! Honk! *Let's go! Practice starts in ten minutes. Coach will be mad if I'm late. Wait! He won't be mad if I'm practicing my breathing!*

Breathe in deep. Count 1, 2, 3. Breathe out slow. And soon I'll go!

Come on, Buster. Think. Think. Imagine your flash cards! The Kansas Speedway is in the state of_________. Ugh!

Think! Think! What would Coach say? I know!

Breathe in deep. Count 1, 2, 3. Breathe out slow. Do your best and go!